It's Shofar Time!

Latifa Berry Kropf

photographs by Tod Cohen

KAR-BEN
PUBLISHING

Thank you . . .

Thanks, as always, to the Congregation Beth Israel Preschool staff and parents.

Special thanks to the children with their sweet neshamas.

—L.B.K.

Dedicated . . .

To the peacemakers, so that all children will grow up into a world of peace and plenty for all.

—L.B.K.

Kar-Ben Publishing, Inc.
A division of Lerner Publishing Group, Inc.
241 First Avenue North
Minneapolis, MN 55401 U.S.A.
1-800-4-KARBEN

Website address: www.karben.com

Library of Congress Cataloging-in-Publication Data

Kropf, Latifa Berry.
    It's shofar time / by Latifa Berry Kropf ; photographs by Tod Cohen.
        p.   cm.
    ISBN-13: 978-1-58013-158-2 (lib. bdg. : alk. paper)
    ISBN-10: 1-58013-158-1 (lib. bdg. : alk. paper)
        1. Rosh ha-Shanah—Juvenile literature. 2. Shofar—Juvenile literature. I. Cohen, Tod. II. Title.
    BM695.N5K76 2006
    296.4'315—dc22   2005009019

Manufactured in the United States of America
3 4 5 6 7 8 – JR – 12 11 10 09 08 07

It's fall. Time to go back to school.
Time to celebrate Rosh Hashanah.

Rosh Hashanah is shofar time. We blow
the shofar to announce the New Year.

A new year is a time to learn new things.
Evan is learning to tie his shoes.

Reuven and Chloe have learned
to write their names.

Look how tall Adam has grown!

The cards we are making for our grandparents
say *"Shanah Tovah"*—"Have a good year."

We bake round challah . . .

And dip apples in honey for a sweet new year.

On Rosh Hashanah it's fun to try new foods.

Denise is tasting a juicy red pomegranate.

Elijah says the star fruit tastes
sweet and sour at the same time.

On the new year we like to wear
our new clothes to synagogue.

Even the Torah wears a special white cover.

We walk to a pond and throw crumbs in the water. This is called *tashlich*.

We pretend the crumbs are things we are sorry we did. We promise to do better this year.

Our favorite part of Rosh Hashanah is hearing the shofar. The first sound is *Tekiyah*—Listen!

Shevarim! Get ready for the new year!

Teruah! Let's make this year a good one!

Tekiah Gedolah! It's fun to blow the longest note with this long shofar.

Shanah Tovah! Happy New Year!

Shofar Craft

What you need:
construction paper
yarn or shoelace
hole punch
markers, crayons, glitter
glue and tape
decorating scraps
party horns

What you do:
Trace a shofar shape on two pieces of construction paper. Cut out both pieces and put one on top of the other. Punch holes around the edges of both.

Sew the pieces together with a shoe lace or piece of yarn taped at one end to form a "needle." Decorate both sides together with crayons, markers, glitter, and/or decorating scraps. Cut the mouth piece from a party horn and tape inside the shofar.

About Rosh Hashanah

Rosh Hashanah celebrates the beginning of the Jewish New Year, which occurs in the fall. Families celebrate at home and in the synagogue. At festive meals, apples and honey are eaten to symbolize the wish for a sweet new year. The Rosh Hashanah *challah* (braided holiday bread) is round to symbolize the cycle of the year. In synagogue, the *shofar*—a ram's horn—is sounded to "awaken" people to think about the year that has passed and the need to change and do better in the year ahead. Special prayers are recited, and the *Torah* (the Five Books of Moses) is read. The traditional holiday greeting is *shanah tovah*, "a good year."

Rosh Hashanah begins a ten-day period of prayer and contemplation ending with Yom Kippur, the Day of Atonement, a solemn day of prayer and fasting.

About the Author

Latifa Berry Kropf has enjoyed teaching children since she started a summer nursery school in her parents' basement as a ten-year-old. She also loves to dance and sing, bake, and do art projects. She has a great husband and two wonderful, mostly grown-up children.

About the Photographer

Tod Cohen is a professional Day-in-the-Life photographer specializing in family and event photography. He loves working with children. Tod lives in Charlottesville, VA, with his two children, Gemma and Henry.